FORSAKEN

YANILIZ NEGRÓN

FORSAKEN

Author: Yaniliz Negron

1

HATEFUL BEGINNINGS

I moved silently through the forest, a shadow weaving seamlessly between the thick trunks and lush undergrowth. The night air was heavy, filled with scents that only my heightened senses could distinguish—damp earth, crisp pine needles, and the subtle aroma of prey somewhere ahead. My paws struck the ground softly, each step precise, each movement calculated. My fur was dark gray, rich and deep like storm clouds at dusk, with soft white streaking along my chest and underbelly. As a wolf shifter, stealth and power were my birthrights. But even more than that, my existence was marked by a profound solitude, one I preferred above all else.

I paused, ears erect, listening intently. A distant rustle alerted me, and I instantly shifted my stance, crouching low, the sleek muscles beneath my fur tensing. The world was simpler this way—free of human pretenses and manipulations. Humans. My lip curled into a silent snarl at the mere thought. Weak, selfish, driven by endless greed. My disdain wasn't baseless; it was carved from painful memories and scars that ran far deeper than my flesh.

Long ago, I'd learned trust was a luxury I could ill afford. I had been betrayed, used, and cast aside by the very species that claimed superiority over nature yet failed to understand the simplest truths of loyalty and honor. I had seen their cities grow, swallowing forests and corrupting rivers. Their pollution poisoned the skies and waters, their presence a disease spreading unchecked. They destroyed everything they touched, oblivious to the balance they disrupted. I hated them for it.

My stomach growled, pulling my thoughts back to the present. Tonight's hunt was necessary, a primal need to feed, survive, and thrive far from their tainted civilization. With renewed determination, I surged forward, swiftly closing the distance to my prey. The scent of a deer was fresh, unmistakable. My heart raced with anticipation, and in mere moments, I spotted the creature—a large buck grazing unsuspectingly in a moonlit clearing.

I crept forward, my senses sharp, each muscle coiled like a spring ready to unleash deadly force. In that instant, I felt perfectly attuned to the wild. This was life in its purest form, survival of the fittest, untouched by human interference. With a powerful burst, I sprang from my hiding spot, covering the ground between us in a heartbeat. The deer bolted, instincts propelling it forward, but I was quicker, stronger. My jaws closed around its neck, delivering swift mercy.

As the life drained from the creature beneath me, a sudden unease prickled my spine. Something was wrong. Instinct warned me before I understood why. A sound—a faint metallic click—pierced the night's serenity. My head snapped up, ears swiveling, searching for the threat. The wind shifted suddenly, bringing an acrid scent that burned my nostrils.

Humans.

The realization hit me seconds too late. Bright lights exploded around the clearing, disorienting and blinding. Pain sliced into my side, sharp and biting, as a trap clamped down, tearing through flesh and muscle. I howled in agony, rage fueling my struggle as I desperately twisted, attempting to break free. Another sharp sting struck my shoulder—a dart or bullet, I couldn't tell amidst the confusion.

"Got him!" I heard a voice shout triumphantly from beyond the blinding lights.

My vision blurred, blood pumping furiously in my ears. The human voices grew louder, the stench of their sweat and adrenaline overwhelming. Fear surged, mingling dangerously with fury. I refused to become their victim, their trophy. Summoning every ounce of strength left in me, I lashed out, jaws snapping furiously, claws tearing at the metal teeth embedded in my flank.

With a final, desperate jerk, I broke free, ripping flesh in the process, my blood spilling onto the forest floor. Pain radiated through every nerve, blinding me with a haze of red. I staggered away, driven solely by instinct and a raw determination not to fall.

"Don't let him escape!" another voice shouted, panicked and angry.

My legs buckled beneath me as I limped forward, each step agony. I pushed myself onward, senses dulling rapidly. Something struck my head, a brutal force that sent stars exploding across my vision. My consciousness wavered dangerously, reality fading in and out.

Somehow, through sheer desperation, I kept moving, stumbling forward, weaving drunkenly through the trees. My mind clouded, memories scattered like leaves in a violent storm. Who was I? What was happening? The scent of blood—my blood—filled the air, guiding me nowhere. Each breath became a Herculean effort, each heartbeat weaker than the last.

Minutes dragged into hours, or perhaps mere seconds stretched into eternity. My thoughts fragmented, disjointed visions flashing through my mind—images of betrayal, pain, solitude. Voices echoed, distant yet familiar, taunting my confusion.

I continued dragging myself forward until, at last, the trees parted, revealing a dark, deserted road. Unable to hold on any longer, my legs gave way beneath me. I collapsed heavily onto the hard, unforgiving asphalt, the darkness pulling at me, wrapping its cold embrace around my battered form. The world slipped from my grasp, fading into nothingness as I drifted into unconsciousness, uncertain if I would ever wake again.

2

A FRAIL SAVIOR

The night had always comforted me. The quiet, the stillness—no people bustling about, no judging eyes. Just the hum of the engine beneath my palms and the stars overhead. My shift at the diner had run late again, and exhaustion settled deep into my bones.

I didn't mind.

There wasn't much waiting for me at home.

Most people didn't understand the kind of loneliness that follows you even when someone shares your house. I had learned that the hard way.

Years ago, I had been in a darker place. Broken in more ways than one. My parents gone. Debts piling higher than I could handle. No real family to lean on. I was young, desperate, and scrambling to stay afloat. That's when I met Freddy.

He was older. Confident. At first, he seemed like a lifeline — a man who noticed me when no one else had. He had money, connections. He promised safety and support. And for a while, he delivered. He paid off my debt collectors. Gave me a place to stay. Put food on the table. It was more than I thought I deserved at the time.

But kindness from men like Freddy always came with conditions.

As soon as the ink on my debts dried, the mask slipped. He became possessive. Controlling. Quick to anger. The first time he hit me, he swore it would never happen again. That he had just been stressed. That he loved me. And I wanted so badly to believe him because I didn't know where else to go.

I had nowhere else to go.

And the hitting never stopped.

Now, years later, things were… tolerable, most days. Freddy spent long stretches away on business trips. He liked control but hated monotony. His absences were my only real freedom.

Like tonight.

With him gone, the house would be quiet when I got home. No harsh words. No judging looks. Just me, the creaking walls, and the ache of another long shift endured.

The thought didn't bring me joy, but it brought relief.

I tightened my grip on the steering wheel as headlights swept across the road ahead. The town had emptied hours ago, leaving only the cold night air and the stretch of asphalt between the diner and home.

I was so tired my bones ached.

As I drove the winding backroads toward my little house tucked near the forest's edge, headlights cut a path through the darkness. The radio played softly, a song about lost chances and fragile hope. Fitting.

Then, something on the roadside caught my eye.

At first, I thought it was just debris. But the shape was too large. Too still. My breath hitched as I slowed the car, pulling over onto the gravel shoulder. My frail hands tightened on the steering wheel for a moment before I forced myself to release them.

A wolf.

It lay sprawled against the asphalt, blood darkening the fur along its side. The sheer size of it made my heart pound. This wasn't a normal wolf. Not by a long shot. Its body rose and fell shallowly—still alive, but barely.

Fear prickled at my skin. Every instinct screamed at me to get back in the car. To drive away.

But something stronger surged up.

Compassion.

"Oh no," I whispered, shoving the door open. The cold night air bit at my face as I stepped out, but I barely felt it.

I hesitated by the door, hands trembling.

Don't, Freddy's voice echoed in my head. *It's just an animal. It's not your problem. Keep walking. Always keep walking.*

And I always had.

So many times over the years, I'd forced myself to turn away. Injured strays on the roadside. Starving kittens behind the diner. Even once, a dog was whimpering in a parking lot with a broken leg. Freddy made it clear from the start—my kindness was weakness. Helping animals was a waste of time and money. "We can't afford to be bleeding hearts," he used to sneer.

I had listened because I had no choice.

But not this time.

Not tonight.

Freddy wasn't here. His judgment wasn't here. Only me. And this wolf.

The closer I got, the more the damage became clear. Deep wounds marred the animal's flank. Blood matted the fur. One of his legs twisted unnaturally. His breaths were shallow, ragged.

I should call someone, I thought.

But who? Animal control? Hunters? They wouldn't help him. They'd probably put him down or worse—treat him like some prize.

I dropped to my knees beside the creature. "Hey, hey... it's okay. I'm not going to hurt you."

My voice trembled. Not from fear of him, but fear that I was already too late.

The wolf's golden eyes opened a fraction. Even through the pain, they burned with something... intelligent. As though he could see straight through me, past the frailty and the fear, down to the stubborn, reckless kindness I could never quite suppress.

"I can't leave you here." I bit my lip. "I don't know if you can hear me, but you're going to have to trust me."

It was ridiculous, talking to a wolf like this.

But he didn't snarl. Didn't flinch.

I took off my coat and draped it gently over his shoulders. "Just hold on, okay?"

The next part was a nightmare.

I wasn't strong. Years of illness had left me fragile, easily exhausted. But adrenaline was a strange thing. Inch by agonizing inch, I managed to pull the wolf toward the car. My muscles screamed in protest. I had to pause more than once, leaning my forehead against his fur, gasping for breath.

"We're almost there," I whispered hoarsely. "Don't give up on me now."

Finally, I hauled him into the backseat with one last desperate effort. His weight almost crushed me. I slid behind the wheel, wiped the sweat from my brow, and started the car.

There was only one person I could turn to.

***

"You did what?"

Anthuan's voice was somewhere between disbelief and exasperation.

"I found him on the road," I said, panting as I pushed open the vet clinic's back door. "He's in bad shape, Anthuan. I couldn't just leave him."

Anthuan ran a hand through his sandy blonde hair. His thin frame always made him seem taller than he was, and the large glasses shadowing his sharp blue eyes gave him a thoughtful, bookish air. He still wore the same beat-up leather jacket from our school days. We had known each other since childhood, our bond forged through years of shared struggles and quiet understanding, though his face had taken on the weariness of someone who'd seen too much. "Isadora... he's a wild animal."

"Please," I begged. "Just look at him. If anyone can save him, it's you."

He hesitated, then sighed. "Fine. Bring him in."

It took everything I had left to help Anthuan get the wolf onto the examination table. Anthuan leaned over him, brow furrowed in concentration.

"This... this isn't normal," he muttered. "The size alone... he's bigger than any wolf I've treated. And these wounds... they're from traps, but he survived things that should've killed him outright."

"So you can help him?"

Anthuan looked up, and for the first time, his stern expression softened. "I'll do my best. For you."

Relief washed over me so powerfully that my knees nearly gave out. "Thank you."

As Anthuan prepared his instruments, I stayed by the wolf's side, resting a trembling hand gently on his uninjured fur. "You're going to make it," I whispered. "I don't care what it takes. I'm not giving up on you."

The wolf's eyes flickered open again. They locked onto mine with an intensity that sent a shiver down my spine.

He didn't know it yet.

But neither was I.

3

HEALING

I awoke to the sharp, sterile scent of antiseptics and unfamiliar voices. My entire body ached, as though fire had seared through my veins. Weakness clung to me like a second skin. Instinct demanded I rise, run, fight. But when I tried to move, agony shot through my side and leg, forcing a strangled whimper from my throat. I could hear the sound of animals around.

Panic surged.

Where was I?

My eyes snapped open, adjusting to the harsh artificial light. The walls were pale, sterile. Machines hummed softly. I was not in the forest. Not in my territory.

Humans.

The scent was unmistakable. Fear, sweat, the sharp tang of their strange medicines. My breath quickened, chest heaving with the effort. I was surrounded. Vulnerable. Caged.

But as the fog in my mind cleared, I realized something even worse. I couldn't shift. The connection to my human form—the bridge between the wild and the civilized—was gone. It was as if the very force that had defined me had been stripped away. A bitter sarcasm, no doubt, from whatever cruel force governed fate. The world is conspiring against me, punishing me for my hatred toward humans.

And that hatred was not without reason. It had shaped me. Defined me.

Humans feared what they couldn't understand. They hunted the unnatural, the extraordinary. They couldn't comprehend beings like me.

Once, I had trusted a human. Believed in her compassion. And when my nature was revealed, she had recoiled. Turned away. Abandoned me. Just as the rest of her kind had done.

Now, fate had twisted the knife deeper. Left me trapped in the form that humans feared most.

The connection to my human form—the part of me that bridged the wild and the civilized—was severed. It was like reaching for a limb that no longer existed.

Panic twisted into rage. I bared my teeth and attempted to stand, but my legs betrayed me, trembling and weak. The slightest motion sent fresh waves of pain rippling through my battered body.

Footsteps approached. I stilled, senses sharpened despite my injuries.

Two figures entered the room. The woman... and the man. The same humans who had found me. My memory flickered like a dying flame, fragments of the roadside, her hands pulling me to safety. Her scent—clean, soft, tinged with earth and wildflowers— lingered in the air.

The man spoke first. "Vitals are steady. That's a good sign."

His voice was calm but carried a note of curiosity. His frame was thin, his sandy blonde hair tousled, large glasses casting shadows over perceptive blue eyes.

The woman, petite, fragile, but with eyes full of determination, hovered near the table. "How's he doing today, Anthuan?" she asked softly, turning to him.

"Better than expected," the man replied. "His wounds are healing fast. Too fast, honestly. I've never seen anything like it."

"That's good, right?" she asked, her voice tinged with hope.

"It's... remarkable. But it raises questions." Anthuan adjusted his glasses and leaned in to examine my side. "Most wolves wouldn't survive injuries like these."

She exhaled slowly and reached into a bag. "I brought him some food."

I tensed as she produced a piece of meat, fresh and raw. Hunger gnawed at me, but I refused to take food from human hands. I growled softly, baring my fangs.

She didn't flinch. Instead, she knelt beside me. "I know you're scared. You've been through hell. But you're safe now. I promise."

Safe? No. This was captivity. Dependence. Everything I had despised and avoided. Yet even as I resented her, a strange warmth stirred inside me—a confusing, unwelcome sensation. Her voice stirred something unfamiliar in me. It wasn't the tone predators used to soothe prey. It wasn't pity either. It was... sincere.

As she leaned closer, I noticed how her brown eyes gleamed in the light, almost a rich caramel color that softened her determined expression. Her light brown hair cascaded softly behind her back, loose strands framing her face with effortless grace. Her features were simple but beautiful, the kind that spoke of quiet resilience rather than vanity. A pair of cat-like glasses rested on her nose, giving her a thoughtful, gentle air.

"Isadora," Anthuan said gently. "Be careful."

My ears perked up at the sound of her name.

Isadora.

"He seems calmer around me," she replied, placing the meat within my reach but not forcing it. "I think he's starting to trust us."

Trust.

A foolish human concept.

Still, hunger gnawed at my insides. Against my better judgment, I tore into the meat. She smiled faintly, the shadows beneath her eyes deepening with relief.

Day after day, the same pattern repeated.

Isadora visited every morning and evening. She spoke to me as though I understood her words. Her hands were gentle, her touch light as she cleaned my wounds and set fresh bandages. The scent of her filled the room, pushing back the cold sterility of the clinic.

Anthuan remained vigilant but respectful, never treating me as a mere beast. His eyes held questions. I could sense the calculations behind them.

Late one evening, I overheard them speaking while they thought I slept.

"He's not like any wolf I've encountered," Anthuan said, voice low. "The rate of healing, the muscle density, even the intelligence in his eyes... It's uncanny. Almost..."

"Almost what?" Isadora whispered.

"Almost human."

The word struck me like a blow. I closed my eyes, feigning sleep. They couldn't know. They *mustn't* know.

I tried to remind myself of all the reasons I hated their kind. Their destruction. Their betrayals. But each day in their presence chipped away at my certainty.

One morning, as Isadora changed my bandages, her fingers brushed against my fur longer than necessary.

"I named you Iskandar," she said softly. "It means 'defender of mankind.' It felt... fitting. Even if you don't believe it yet."

Iskandar.

I almost growled at the irony. A name tying me to the very species I loathed.

But as her fingertips lingered with care I didn't deserve, I couldn't bring myself to reject it.

Instead, I watched her. Studied her. Learned the cadence of her voice, the subtle weariness in her smile. Her hands bore small scars—proof of past struggles. She was no predator. No threat.

She was... something else.

I didn't want to understand. But I was beginning to.

And that frightened me more than any trap or bullet ever had.

4

THE BOND

The days blurred into a quiet, repetitive rhythm. The sterile clinic had become a strange sanctuary, but also a prison. My strength returned gradually, the fire in my muscles reigniting as my wounds closed faster than either Anthuan or Isadora could explain. Still, I couldn't shift. The bridge to my human form remained broken, a constant, gnawing reminder of my vulnerability.

Isadora's visits became the constant I begrudgingly relied on. Her soft voice. The gentle touch of her fingers. The scent of wildflowers and warm earth seemed to cling to her every time she entered the room. She never forced closeness, yet her presence filled the space more than any cage or wall.

But things were changing. The clinic wasn't home for either of us.

***

"Anthuan," Isadora said one evening, "he's too big to stay here much longer. I can't let him live like this."

Anthuan frowned, arms crossed, glasses slipping down his nose. "Isadora… he's not a pet. He's a wild animal. You've done more than anyone else would."

"He's not just any animal," she argued gently but firmly. "I can feel it. There's something more to him. I can't explain it."

I listened from the corner of the room, pretending to sleep. Her words struck something deep inside me. Something dangerous.

Anthuan sighed heavily. "What will Freddy say when he finds a wolf in your house? You've kept him away for weeks now, but he'll be back soon."

Freddy.

The name stirred a low, instinctive growl in my throat. I'd never met him, but even hearing his name filled me with unease.

"I'll handle Freddy," Isadora replied. Her voice was calm, but a shadow crossed her caramel eyes.

Anthuan's gaze hardened. "That's what you always say. But what if he reacts dangerously? What if it's like the last time?"

Isadora's shoulders tensed. "It won't happen again."

"Izzy." His voice softened, using the childhood name he rarely spoke now. "It shouldn't have happened the first time. You shouldn't even be with him."

She looked away, arms wrapping around herself. "I can handle it."

"No. You survive it. That's not the same." Anthuan's blue eyes flashed behind his glasses. "I've seen the scars, Isadora. Don't pretend I haven't. You hide them like they don't exist, but I see them every time you pull away from a touch."

Silence stretched between them.

"I didn't say anything before because I thought maybe things would change," he continued. "But they haven't. And now you've brought someone vulnerable into the house. If Freddy lashes out—at the wolf or at you—I won't stand by."

Her voice wavered. "I'm not asking you to."

Anthuan removed his glasses and pinched the bridge of his nose. "I trust you, Izzy. But I don't trust him. And neither should you."

"I promise I'll be careful."

"You've always been stubborn."

"Always."

***

Moving me wasn't easy. Even with Anthuan's help, Isadora strained under the effort, her frailty evident in every trembling muscle. Yet she refused to let me walk alone or be transported like cargo. She insisted on being part of every moment.

Her home was small but warm. The scent of herbs and old books filled the air. She had prepared a space in the living room, soft blankets layered across the floor beside a fireplace.

"It's not much," she whispered as she guided me inside, "but it's yours for now."

I resisted the urge to retreat. The closeness to humans—their scents, their sounds—was suffocating. But when she placed her hand on my head, scratching gently behind my ears, some primal tension eased.

Days passed.

One night, something changed.

I lay stretched near the fireplace, the warmth easing the lingering ache in my leg. Isadora moved through the house, believing me asleep. I wasn't.

She entered her bedroom and left the door slightly ajar. My sharp ears caught the soft rustle of clothing. Curiosity—an old, dangerous habit—stirred in me. I shifted my head just enough to glimpse through the crack.

Isadora stood by the dresser, her back to me. She peeled off her shirt and jeans with slow, tired motions. Her body wasn't the flawless, airbrushed beauty humans seemed to worship. She had average breasts, a soft curve to her belly, and wide hips that balanced her delicate frame. But to my eyes, there was allure in every line and shape. Strength in her softness.

Yet it wasn't desire that froze me.

It was the scars.

One long scar traced her ribs. Another marred the back of her shoulder. The third, a pale slash, crossed her clavicle.

My breath caught. A silent snarl rose within me—not at her, but at the implications.

She always moved carefully, always rubbed her side when she thought no one noticed. These weren't the marks of accidents or careless injuries. They told a story of pain, of survival.

I hated the thoughts that surfaced. Hated the image of that man—Freddy—who I had yet to meet, but whose scent already triggered my instincts. From the way Anthuan spoke of him, from Isadora's constant deflections and calm words hiding something deeper, I suspected Freddy was no gentle presence in her life.

I lowered my head back to my paws, muscles tight.

The desire to protect her was becoming something sharp. Something dangerous.

I began to understand that hatred wasn't the only emotion that burned in me anymore.

Her kindness wasn't weakness.

It was defiance. The stubborn refusal to let life's hardships make her cruel or bitter.

And I watched. And learned.

The next evening, as the light from the fireplace cast flickering shadows across the room, she brought fresh bandages and a small brush. I expected Anthuan, but it was only her tonight.

"Let's get these changed, handsome," she murmured with a smile, kneeling beside me. Her breath was a little labored from the effort, but her hands were steady.

She carefully peeled away the old wrappings, her fingers brushing my fur with delicate precision. The wounds had nearly closed, yet she treated them as if they were still raw. As if I was still fragile.

I stiffened out of habit. Everything in me screamed to pull away. To snarl. To keep the barrier firm between her world and mine.

But her touch was warm. Gentle.

She finished the dressings, then picked up the brush. "This might help you relax. Anthuan said it would keep your coat healthy. I hope... you don't mind."

I watched her cautiously as she brought the bristles to my fur. The first stroke was tentative. Light. Testing.

Instinct made my lip twitch. A low growl coiled in my throat—but it didn't rise.

Instead, a surprising comfort washed over me. The rhythm of the brush through my fur was calming, her fingers steady even as her breath wavered with fatigue. No fear. No dominance. Just care.

"You're not as scary as you want people to believe," she whispered with a soft laugh.

I closed my eyes, the tension in my muscles easing. The world had taught me that humans brought pain, fear, and betrayal.

But this one... this human... was teaching me something else entirely.

5

PROTECTOR

The night was quiet but not silent. Outside, the forest whispered with the sounds of nocturnal life. Inside, the warmth of the small house wrapped around me—a comfort I never thought I'd associate with a human dwelling.

My legs had grown stronger. The lingering aches were a distant memory now. I had tested my weight quietly for days, cautious, never wanting to alarm her.

Tonight, I moved.

I rose slowly from my place by the fireplace, careful not to disturb the soft blankets she had laid out for me. My paws made no sound as they pressed against the worn floorboards.

I paused at the bedroom door.

Isadora slept curled beneath a thin blanket. The moonlight spilled across her face, highlighting the soft waves of her light brown hair cascading across the pillow. Her caramel eyes were closed in a peaceful expression I rarely saw during waking hours. Shadows underlined her eyes—shadows earned from exhaustion, long shifts, and worries she never spoke aloud.

Her features were simple but beautiful, even now. Vulnerable.

I watched for a moment longer, then slipped away into the rest of the house.

The space was small but filled with her essence. Herbs hung drying by the window. The scent of old books mingled with the ever-present trace of wildflowers clinging to her belongings.

I explored quietly, noting the simple furnishings. The dining table was cluttered with unopened mail, a pair of cracked mugs, and a chipped ceramic bowl half-filled with coins and keys.

Over time, I had learned her patterns.

She worked long shifts and at odd hours. When she returned, her scent was always touched with grease and cooking oil—a clear mark of someone working at a restaurant or food chain.

Yet no matter how tired she looked, no matter how late it was, her eyes brightened the instant she saw me.

Every night, she would drop her bag and whatever else she carried onto the dining table. Then she would kneel beside me, smile wide, and scratch gently behind my ears.

"Hey, handsome. Miss me?" she would say.

Her joy seemed genuine, as if seeing me was the highlight of her day.

She spoiled me—without hesitation. Treats, fresh meat, anything she could afford. I noticed her meals were often simple. Canned soup, boxed noodles, or cheap takeout. Yet for me, she always found the best.

Once fed and changed into comfortable clothes, she would settle down beside me. Always with a book in hand. The titles varied—sometimes fantasy, sometimes historical romance. She had a habit of reading aloud small passages, as though sharing the stories with me.

And slowly, talking to me had become a habit.

"You know," she said one evening, legs tucked beneath her, "Anthuan thinks I'm crazy. Keeping you here. Trusting you. But I can't explain it... I feel like you understand me in a way no one else does."

I listened, head resting on my paws, eyes half-closed. My instincts told me not to grow attached. Not to blur the line between creature and caretaker.

But instincts were losing the battle.

Her voice filled the space between us night after night. She told me about her childhood with Anthuan. Her dreams before life became burdened with responsibility. Her love for animals, for quiet nights and old stories.

I was no longer just observing her.

I was learning to know her.

And every day, the hatred that once defined me unraveled a little more.

But I couldn't ignore the truth forever.

One night, when the house had grown silent and Isadora's soft breaths drifted from the bedroom, I ventured farther than before. Past the living room. Down the narrow hallway. My claws clicked softly on the floorboards as I approached the bathroom door, which she always left slightly open.

The mirror above the sink reflected my wolf form. Strong. Whole. But incomplete.

I closed my eyes and reached deep into myself. Searching for that connection—the tether to my human shape. The bridge I had once crossed so easily.

I felt nothing.

Growling low, I tried again. I pictured my hands, my voice, my face. Willed the shift to begin.

Agony lanced through me. My bones trembled beneath fur and flesh. For a moment, the sensation of change stirred, like a spark threatening to catch flame.

Then it died.

I collapsed onto the cool tile floor, panting. My claws scraped the ceramic in frustration.

"Damn it," I snarled under my breath—a sound only I could understand.

Was this it? Was I meant to remain like this forever? A creature bound to instincts, unable to reclaim the man I once was?

The logical choice whispered through my mind: *Leave. Leave before it's too late. Before you hurt her. Before you grow too attached.*

But as I turned toward the door, ready to slip away into the shadows of the forest beyond, an image stopped me.

Her face.

Isadora's soft smile when she returned home each night. The joy in her caramel eyes when she greeted me. The way her weariness seemed to vanish the moment our eyes met.

If I left now, would she search for me? Would she worry? Would she wonder if she had done something wrong?

A sharp ache pierced deeper than any physical wound. I had lost many things before. Family. Friends. Trust. But the thought of leaving her—*abandoning* her—felt like a fresh betrayal I couldn't stomach.

Coward.

I returned to the living room, settling onto the blanket she had prepared for me. As I lay my head down, her scent surrounded me, grounding the tempest inside.

For now... I would stay.

The days that followed became a strange, quiet routine I had never imagined myself accepting.

When Isadora came home each evening, I found myself rising to greet her before I even thought about it. My tail—traitorous thing—began to wag with each click of the lock and creak of the door. I cursed under my breath in my mind, berating myself for such a pathetic display of domestication.

Yet when she saw me, her entire face would light up.

"Oh! Look at you!" she'd squeal in delight, tossing her things onto the table and rushing over. "You missed me, didn't you?"

Before I could even brace myself, she'd wrap her arms around my neck and press her face into my fur. "Good boy. You're such a good boy."

I wanted to snarl. To pull away. But the warmth of her embrace had become something I could no longer resist.

Fool, I thought. You're not some domesticated mutt.

But the wagging tail always betrayed me.

***

One particularly cold night, after she had fed me and eaten her usual cheap dinner, I noticed something unsettling. As she settled into bed, the thin blanket she pulled over herself was barely enough to ward off the chill. Her body shivered beneath it.

I glanced back at the nest of blankets and soft sheets she had prepared for me beside the fireplace—the best linens she owned, no doubt.

She had given me the best.

And kept the worst for herself.

For several minutes, I lay there, torn between pride and instinct.

Then instinct won.

Quiet as a shadow, I padded down the hallway. She stirred slightly as I pushed open the bedroom door with my snout.

"Iskandar?" she mumbled sleepily.

I hesitated. This was foolish. Dangerous. Unwise.

But the sight of her shivering beneath the threadbare blanket broke whatever stubbornness I had left.

With deliberate steps, I climbed onto the bed and curled beside her. My larger frame pressed against her back, my fur trapping the heat between us.

"Just to keep you warm," I told myself silently. "That's all."

But deep down, I knew the truth.

I liked her company. I liked her nearness. And for once in my long, cursed life, I didn't want to be alone.

She sighed softly and leaned into me, her shivering ceasing almost at once. "Thank you," she whispered, not fully awake.

I closed my eyes, prepared to remain still until she fell fully back asleep.

But then she stirred again.

Slowly, with the trust only deep sleep could grant, Isadora rolled toward me. Her arms wrapped gently around my broad neck, her face nestling into the thick fur of my chest. I stiffened instinctively at first—trained by years of solitude to reject closeness.

But the scent of her hair, the soft rise and fall of her breath, melted my resistance. My muscles relaxed.

She sighed in contentment, the tension leaving her body as if my presence had chased away not just the cold, but also the weight of whatever burdens haunted her waking hours.

Then, in a soft murmur barely audible over the quiet hum of the night, she whispered, "You're the best thing that has happened to me, Iskandar."

The words struck deeper than any wound I had suffered.

I swallowed hard—not that she could see. She wouldn't know that those simple, sleepy words unraveled what little remained of my barriers.

The wolf in me urged retreat. Warned that this was dangerous, that letting a human inside my heart was a path to pain.

But I didn't move.

I couldn't.

Because in that fragile, unguarded moment, I realized something terrifying.

I didn't want to be just her protector.

I wanted to stay.

6

TRANSFORMATION

It was late when he returned.

I caught his scent before he ever crossed the threshold—cheap cologne masking sweat and the heavy stench of alcohol. The reek of dominance and anger clung to him like a second skin. My lip curled instinctively.

Freddy.

The man she had mentioned, but whom I had never fully encountered. Until now.

The front door burst open without warning. Heavy boots stomped across the worn floorboards. A short, stocky man with a small, unshaven beard and shaggy black hair filled the doorway. His gut pressed against the buttons of his jacket. His eyes—dark and bloodshot—searched the room with the expectation of being greeted like royalty.

But instead of dinner waiting on the table and Isadora rushing to meet him, he found her lounging on the floor beside me. A book open in her lap. Her caramel eyes alight with laughter as she read aloud to me.

Freddy's expression darkened instantly.

"What the hell is this?" he barked, gesturing wildly.

Isadora's smile faltered. "Freddy, you're home early. I—"

"Damn right I'm home early! And what do I find? No food. No greeting. Just you giggling like a fool with a wolf."

He stormed toward us, his boots loud and heavy. My muscles tensed. Instinct screamed to rise, to snarl, to defend.

"Freddy, please," Isadora stood quickly, hands raised. "It's not what you think. He's still recovering. I was just—"

"I don't give a damn what you were doing," he snapped, his voice slurred from drink. "You've been hiding this beast from me for weeks. Feeding him. Letting him sleep in the house. Are you insane?"

He pointed a shaking, meaty finger at me. "That thing goes. Tonight."

I rose slowly to my full height, fur bristling, ears pinned back. My tail held high, not in submission but in warning.

"Freddy, please!" Isadora stepped between us, pressing her hands against his chest. "He's not dangerous. I promise."

"Not dangerous?" Freddy's hand lashed out.

The crack echoed in the small house.

Isadora stumbled back, one hand flying to her reddening cheek.

Something inside me snapped.

I surged forward, a deep, guttural snarl ripping from my throat. My teeth bared fully for the first time since the attack in the forest.

Freddy stumbled back in surprise. His eyes, bloodshot and narrowed, widened with sudden fear. "Get that monster away from me!"

But I wasn't moving back.

I positioned myself firmly between him and Isadora, my entire body rigid, ready to strike if he dared lift a hand to her again.

Freddy didn't move.

He didn't understand that the wolf before him was not just an animal. I wasn't her pet. I wasn't tame.

I was a guardian.

And he had just crossed a line he would regret.

In that moment, whatever hatred I once held toward humanity had found a new, singular focus.

I didn't just dislike Freddy.

I loathed him.

Freddy's shock was fleeting. Rage replaced it, dark and suffocating. "Don't you dare growl at me," he hissed.

He grabbed Isadora's arm, yanking her hard against him. She cried out, her free hand clawing at his jacket. "Freddy, let go! You're hurting me!"

My snarl deepened, teeth bared in a silent promise. Release her—or suffer.

"I said shut up!" Freddy roared, shaking her roughly. "This is what happens when you don't listen. When you keep secrets."

Isadora tried to pull away, but Freddy tightened his grip. Bruising fingers dug into the soft flesh of her upper arm. Her eyes met mine over his shoulder—wide, frightened, silently pleading.

That was the last restraint I had.

I lunged forward, placing myself squarely between them, lips curled back over sharp teeth. Freddy's face paled.

"Back off!" he spat, releasing Isadora with a shove that sent her stumbling backward into the table.

Then, moving faster than expected for a man of his bulk, Freddy reached into his duffle bag near the door.

He pulled out a gun.

Cold metal. Black. Heavy.

The click of the safety disengaging was deafening.

"I should've done this the moment I walked in," Freddy sneered, leveling the barrel at me. "I'm done playing around."

Isadora gasped. "Freddy, no! Please, don't!"

She rushed toward him, grasping his arm. "Stop this! He hasn't done anything!"

"Get off me, woman!" Freddy snarled, shoving her aside. But she clung to his wrist desperately, trying to lower the weapon.

The scene burned into my mind. Isadora—frail, stubborn, fearless—risking herself to protect me.

Something inside me snapped. Not with rage.

With purpose.

The shift stirred—violent, agonizing, undeniable. My bones twisted. Muscles stretched, skin tore, and reformed. For a brief moment, I felt as though I were being ripped apart and rebuilt at once.

My vision blurred.

Isadora screamed as Freddy shoved her to the floor and turned the gun toward her.

No.

Time slowed.

I surged forward—human. Flesh, not fur. Naked but powerful. I grabbed Freddy's wrist just as he pulled the trigger.

The gunshot rang out. The bullet slammed into the ceiling.

Freddy's eyes widened in shock as he stared at me—no longer the wolf he'd tried to dominate, but a man. Tanned skin streaked with the remnants of the shift, messy black hair falling into piercing hazel eyes that burned with fury.

"You'll never touch her again," I growled, voice low and cold.

For the first time, Freddy looked truly afraid.

But fear soon twisted into fury. "You're—" he spat, eyes wild. "You're an abomination. A shifter. One of those monsters the hunters are always warning about."

He tried to wrench his arm free, but my grip was iron. He clawed at me with his free hand, fists striking my bare chest with pathetic force.

I didn't even flinch.

"Let me go! I'll call them. I'll call the hunters—"

He twisted, scrambling to grab his phone from the duffle bag.

I moved faster.

My other hand shot out, slamming the phone to the floor where it shattered on impact.

Freddy's breathing grew ragged. Desperation clung to him like sweat. "You can't kill me," he rasped. "The hunters will find you. They'll find her too."

"Stop!" Isadora cried, her voice cracking. She rushed to my side, her small hands pressing against my arm. "Please, Iskandar. Don't kill him."

Her touch grounded me. The fire of adrenaline roared in my veins, but her presence pulled me back from the edge.

I stared Freddy down, my voice a low, dangerous rumble. "You can walk away. Or you can die here. Your choice."

Freddy's gaze darted between us. He sneered, but the terror in his eyes betrayed him. "This isn't over."

He stumbled backward, nearly tripping over the doorframe before bolting into the night.

For several long moments, only the sound of Isadora's breath filled the space between us.

My body trembled—not from fear, but from the sheer force of the transformation and the adrenaline still surging through me.

Slowly, I turned to face her.

Her caramel eyes were wide, lips parted in shock. She took a step back, but didn't run.

She didn't scream.

She didn't look at me like a monster.

I knelt, grabbing one of the blankets from the couch and gently draping it around her shoulders.

But it was she who broke the silence first. A flush crept into her cheeks as her eyes dipped lower.

"You might wanna put some clothes on," she whispered.

Her attempt at humor—fragile, nervous—broke through the heavy tension.

I managed a faint, rough chuckle. "Right."

She handed me the blanket. I stood there; the blanket now draped over me as if it could shield me from the enormity of what had just happened.

"You—" she began, voice trembling. "I knew... you were not just a wolf."

I nodded slowly. "No."

She bit her lip, searching my eyes. "All this time... I knew there was something different. But I thought... maybe I was just imagining it."

"You weren't."

The fear I expected—*dreaded*—never fully appeared in her eyes. There was shock. Confusion. But beneath it, the same stubborn warmth that had drawn me to her from the beginning.

"You saved me," she whispered. "Again."

"And I'll keep saving you," I said, voice hoarse. "If you'll let me."

Her breath hitched. She reached up, fingertips brushing lightly against my jaw. "I already did. Long before tonight."

The weight of the moment settled between us. My instincts told me to back away. To protect her from the danger I had brought into her life. But my heart—a part of me I thought had withered long ago—refused.

"I never wanted this to happen like this," I admitted, the words tasting foreign on my tongue. "I wanted to tell you. But I... I didn't think you'd accept what I am."

"You think after everything, I'd turn you away?" She shook her head, eyes shining. "Iskandar, you've been protecting me since the moment I found you. You've never been the danger in my life. Freddy was."

Her trust—her *belief*—was more terrifying than Freddy's threats, more humbling than any injury I had endured.

I swallowed hard. "I'll stay. If you want me to."

Isadora smiled softly, tears clinging to her lashes. "I want you to stay."

And for the first time since my world had fallen apart, I no longer felt like a creature cursed to wander alone.

I felt... home.

***

In the days that followed, I adjusted to life as a man once more—not because I had to.

Because I wanted to. For her.

The first few days were awkward, to say the least. Clothes were a challenge—Isadora had to dig through every spare drawer to find something that might fit until Anthuan grudgingly lent me a few pieces from his older, larger cousin's wardrobe. The shoes pinched. The jeans were too short. But I endured it all for her.

The hardest part wasn't adjusting to the human world again. It was explaining it.

When Isadora finally gathered the courage to tell Anthuan, she called him over to the house. He arrived expecting a sick animal, not a shirtless man standing awkwardly in the corner with a blanket around his shoulders.

Anthuan froze in the doorway, grocery bag in one hand, glasses sliding halfway down his nose. His sharp blue eyes blinked rapidly as he stared between us.

"This is… Iskandar," Isadora said quietly, chewing her lower lip.

Anthuan looked at her. Then at me. Then back at her. His gaze slowly traveled up my tall frame, taking in the scars, the broad shoulders, the disheveled black hair, and the hazel eyes that had once glared at him from a wolf's face.

He set the grocery bag down carefully—almost reverently. "Isadora… forgive me for asking, but…" He pushed his glasses up. "Where exactly can I find more wolves like this?"

Isadora blinked. "What?"

Anthuan crossed his arms, smirking. "I've been helping you rescue strays for years. And not once has a single one turned into a ridiculously handsome man."

Isadora flushed deep red. "Anthuan!"

I fought the urge to smirk. The tension that had knotted my shoulders since that night eased slightly.

Anthuan sobered, his teasing fading into genuine curiosity. "So… you're a shifter. That explains everything. The healing, the intelligence, the size." His gaze sharpened. "And the protectiveness."

I nodded once. "Yes."

He blew out a slow breath, running a hand through his sandy blonde hair. "Well, hell. That's definitely a first. But…" His eyes softened as they landed on Isadora. "If anyone was going to take in a man-beast and make him civilized, it'd be you."

She smiled, eyes bright. "I didn't civilize him. He chose to stay."

Anthuan grinned, then shot me a warning look. "Good. Because if you hurt her—even as a human—I'll call every hunter in the county. Don't think I won't."

"I have no intention of ever hurting her," I said firmly.

Anthuan gave a satisfied nod. "Then we'll get along just fine."

The human speech felt heavy on my tongue after so long in silence.

But Isadora's soft laughter made it easier.

I stayed close, never straying far from her side. When she went to work, I escorted her, staying nearby without interfering. She had never asked for a protector, but I became one anyway. Watching. Guarding. Ensuring no shadow or stranger threatened the peace she had so tirelessly built.

The locals thought I was her cousin, newly arrived. Anthuan smirked but played along, making sure no rumors spread.

Freddy had disappeared. I doubted he'd risk returning—especially now that he understood what I was. But I remained vigilant.

Nights were the best. We returned home together. The fireplace would crackle, casting golden light across the small living room. She'd cook simple meals, sometimes reading aloud as she had before. But now, I could answer. Laugh. Tease.

We shared the couch, sometimes saying little, sometimes talking until dawn.

One particular evening, the wind howled outside. The temperature had dropped sharply, frost clinging to the edges of the window.

Isadora wrapped a large blanket around our shoulders and pulled me close. "You know," she whispered, head resting against my chest, "this was easier when you were covered in fur."

I smiled, pressing a kiss to her temple. "I think you like me better this way."

She chuckled. "Maybe."

We sat in comfortable silence, the flames reflecting in her caramel eyes.

I tipped her chin up gently, our faces inches apart. "You saved me long before I ever saved you."

Her breath mingled with mine, warm and uneven.

"Then maybe it's time you let me keep doing it."

The vulnerability in her voice struck something raw and deep inside me. She wasn't just offering comfort—she was offering us. A chance neither of us had dared to imagine before.

I cupped her face gently, my thumb tracing the soft curve of her cheek. Her skin was warm beneath my touch, her eyes searching mine not with fear or uncertainty, but with quiet, steadfast trust.

Slowly, I closed the distance between us. Our lips brushed in a feather-light touch that sent a jolt through every nerve in my body. She leaned into me, the tension between us melting away.

The second kiss deepened—slow, deliberate, as though we were both savoring the moment we'd been unconsciously building toward since the night she'd dragged my broken body into her car.

Her hands slid up to my shoulders, fingers gripping the fabric of my shirt like she feared I might vanish. But I wasn't going anywhere. Not now. Not ever.

My arm circled her waist, pulling her closer until there was no space left between us, just shared breath and the rapid beating of our hearts.

The kiss wasn't just passion.

It was a promise.

A surrender.

A beginning.

As the fire warmed us, I realized the truth I had fought so long to deny.

Not all humans were the same.

Some... were worth everything.

END

Puerto Rico is known for its vibrant culture, breathtaking beaches, and rich history. But beneath the beauty lies a growing crisis—the rising population of stray dogs and cats.

Thousands of stray animals—often called *satos*—and countless cats roam the streets, beaches, and forests of Puerto Rico. Many have been abandoned, neglected, or born into a life without shelter or care. They face daily struggles: hunger, disease, abuse, and the harsh elements.

Despite the challenges, countless rescue organizations and compassionate individuals work tirelessly to help. Groups like *Save a Gato*, *Fundacion por los Animales*, and local volunteers dedicate their time and resources to rescue, rehabilitate, and rehome these vulnerable animals. Their work is a testament to human kindness and the belief that every life, no matter how small or voiceless, deserves dignity and love.

But awareness is just as important as action. Stray animals are not just "someone else's problem." They reflect a larger need for responsible pet ownership, accessible spay/neuter programs, and community education.

If you see a stray in need:

Contact a local rescue group for guidance.
Provide water and food if safe to do so.
Advocate for stronger animal welfare policies.

Together, we can change the narrative for Puerto Rico's stray animals—from abandonment to hope. Every act of compassion matters.

Because saving one life may not change the world, but for that one life, the world will change forever.

ACKNOWLEDGMENTS

This story was born one quiet afternoon after bathing my dogs—both rescues—and seeing how genuinely happy, safe, and loved they are now. That moment reminded me how many animals are still out there, waiting for kindness. As someone who loves reading and writing romance and fantasy, I wanted to take that passion and use it to say something more. This short story is my way of giving voice to those who can't speak for themselves. Stray animals, especially in places like Puerto Rico, often suffer due to human negligence. They didn't choose to be abandoned or forgotten—but we can choose to help. Through this story, I hope to share a message of compassion, healing, and the kind of love that can change lives—human and animal alike.

A heartfelt thank you to the friends and rescuers who support this mission, especially Rosana Miranda and the incredible crew of I Love Dogs Inc. Your dedication inspires every word of this story.

ABOUT THE AUTHOR

Yaniliz Negrón, a native of San Juan, Puerto Rico, discovered her love for reading and writing through the Harry Potter books, which also helped her learn English. Fluent in both Spanish and English, Yaniliz has always enjoyed imagining wild ideas and exploring the "what ifs" of everyday life. Her writing journey began with fanfics, which eventually evolved into original stories. Currently, she is working on new ideas and creating her multiverse. She studied Graphic Design and Game Design at Atlantic College. She lives in San Juan with her husband, two kids, two dogs, and seven cats. She loves sharing her worlds and ideas with others. Follow her on social media.

Instagram: @lbynegron